OLD PALACE

OLD PALACE

SHEEBA ALEKSON

Old Palace

Copyright © 2021 by Sheeba Alekson. All rights reserved.

No part of this publication may be reproduced, stored in a retrieval system or transmitted in any way by any means, electronic, mechanical, photocopy, recording or otherwise without the prior permission of the author except as provided by USA copyright law.

The opinions expressed by the author are not necessarily those of URLink Print and Media.

1603 Capitol Ave., Suite 310 Cheyenne, Wyoming USA 82001
1-888-980-6523 | admin@urlinkpublishing.com

URLink Print and Media is committed to excellence in the publishing industry.

Book design copyright © 2021 by URLink Print and Media. All rights reserved.

Published in the United States of America

Library of Congress Control Number: 2021906775
ISBN 978-1-64753-751-7 (Paperback)
ISBN 978-1-64753-752-4 (Digital)

25.03.21

This novel "old palace" is inspired by the real events of Hyderabad city which is located in India. It is the story of spirit of pretty girl who is roaming in city, contacting the unmarried men and proposing her own marriage and offering old palace.

Author's Introduction

I live in Minnesota, USA with my parent, brother and sister. I like watching and reading horror stories since childhood. I was born in India on 24 June 1971 in Hyderabad city which is located in India. I belong to educated and traditional family. I obtained 3 years degree from Osmania University in 1994.

I migrated united states of America in 2012. "Old palace." is my first novel. I started writing novel in 2015.

"Agriculture land"

India is a land of agriculture and historical places. Before independence (1947), there was rule of kings in a different cites of India. Kings used to build the palaces for their living. Some kings used to build palaces for them livings on a very big land. That palace which build on a very big area of land called "Qila". Some kings used to build the palace on a little big area of land. That palace which built on a little big area of land called 'Haveli'. kings used to live in that palaces with their family (wife and children).

"Qila"

Haveli

(PICTURE NOT AVAILABLE)

In India, people of olden age used to say that many ghosts lives in 'Qilas' and 'Havelies', and in agricultural area. Ghost use to dance and sing the songs in "Qilas,' "Havelies," and agricultural land. People who use to pass near the "Havelies" and "Qilas" and agriculture land can hear the songs. People can hear the sound of weeping from Qilas and Havelies. Ghosts use to sing, dance and weep mostly in nights according to the people of old age. Now days also people can see the ghosts and hear the sound of weeping and singing. Mostly there are ghosts of women.

"Hyderabad City"

My grandfather was a Doctor and was working in a village named " Nalgonda," which is located near Hyderabad city. In my childhood, my grandfather retired from his job and came back to Hyderabad city and used to stay with us. He used to tell us the real events of ghosts which ware occurred in his village "Nalgonda ", where he used to work.

In India villages are more, and cities are less. Hyderabad is a city in India where I used to live before migrating to united states of America. My father use d to tell the events of ghosts. He told that he saw many ghosts from his childhood till now. He told that sometimes ghosts use to comes near to him and disappears sometimes. People use to say that more ghosts use to be in villages and less in cities, in India.

"Village of India"

Sheeba Alekson

"City of India"

Old Palace

India got independence in the year 1947. Before independence India was not India. India was not a one country. One king used to rule one or more than one cities including some villages. So, many kings used to rule on different parts of India. Hyderabad including some villages ware ruled by one king. His name was Irfan Ali Khan.

King Irfan Ali Khan built two palaces in Hyderabad for living. One palace called ' Qadeem Haveli' and one palace called Nayi Haveli. Qadeem means old, Haveli means palace so it is old palace. Nayi means new Haveli means palace, so it is new palace. King had two wives or more, I do not know but I know about his two wives. He used to live in two palaces with his two wives and children. He had two sons and one daughter from his first wife. His elder son name was Imran Ali Khan, younger son name was Kamran Ali Khan and daughters name was Princess Shabnam, his wife name was Queen Shakeela. They all used to live in" Old palace."

Part 1

Both the sons of King Irfan Ali Khan ware married and daughter was un married. Bothe sons used to stay in "Old palace" with their wives and children.

After the death of King Irfan Ali Khan, Queen Shakeela and her daughter Princess Shabnam used to live alone with one servant because both the sons of King Irfan Ali Khan left the palace including their wives and children.

The "Old palace" is locked now. I saw it. It is very beautiful. It is near to my house, where I was live before migrating United States of America. Nobody is living in it because Queen Shakeela and Princess Shabnam also died and servant went away from the palace, rest of the family members are now alive? or not? I do not know but, they are not in India. In new palace, his second wife and children used lived, it is also locked but I do not know where are they now.

In 1994, one incident occurs in my city, near to my house. The incident was that one lady ghost was roaming around the city and contacting unmarried boys and telling them "if you marry me I will transfer my Qadeem Haveli on your name." The lady ghost was contacting only the unmarried boys. She was roaming only in nights and seen by unmarried boys. Married men and women could not see her. I was very scared during those days because I heard from somebody that she was roaming from in front of my house also. All the people of city were scared and nobody was going out at night. Only few who do not believe in ghost were going out.

one day a unmarried boy who used to live near to my house saw that lady ghost, while walking on the way after attaining the late-night party in his uncle`s house, when he came near to his house, saw the lady ghost. The time was 2:30 midnight. After seventh day of seeing the lady ghost, he came to my house and told the incident of lady ghost to me and my sister. That young boy named Jugnu.

I and my sister both shocked and started thinking that "How could the boy of so young age face the lady ghost". I think that the age of that boy was 17 or 18 years.

I and my sister stared questioning to him, after hearing the incident of lady ghost. My sister questioned him "How she looked"? Jugnu answered her "She was very pretty. She had big and black eyes, black and long hairs, straight nose. She was very fair, slim, and tall.

I asked Jugnu "What she wore?".

Jugnu said " She wore yellow sharara", and dupatta. She covered her head with dupatta.

Sharara means long blouse and long skirt. Dupatta means scarf. It was the traditional dress of Indians females in olden days. In India females used to covered their heads with dupatta(scarf).

It was the custom of olden days.

My sister (Noorjahan) asked Jugnu "How did you realize that she is a lady ghost not a lady?".

Jugnu said " I realized that she is a lady ghost not a lady because she was communicating me in a horrible manner ".

I shocked and asked him "What she told you?

Jugnu said "she told me that if you marry me I will transfer my" Old Palace" on your name".

"Yellow Sharara"

Sheeba Alekson

I asked Jugnu "What was the time?

Jugnu told "The time was 2;30 night.

I shocked and asked him "what were you doing there at that time "?

Jugnu told "I was returning home after attaining the function which was in my uncle's house.

I questioned him " When did it happen?".

Jugnu answers "Seven days back".

I questioned him "You were alone on the way?".

Jugnu answered "Yes I were alone on the way

I asked Jugnu "What did you realize on the way?".

Jugnu told "I realized that some body is following me and I am continuously hearing some sound.

I asked Jugnu " what kind of sound?".

Jugnu told " The sound was "Chan" "Chan" "Chan" "Chan"

"Pazab"

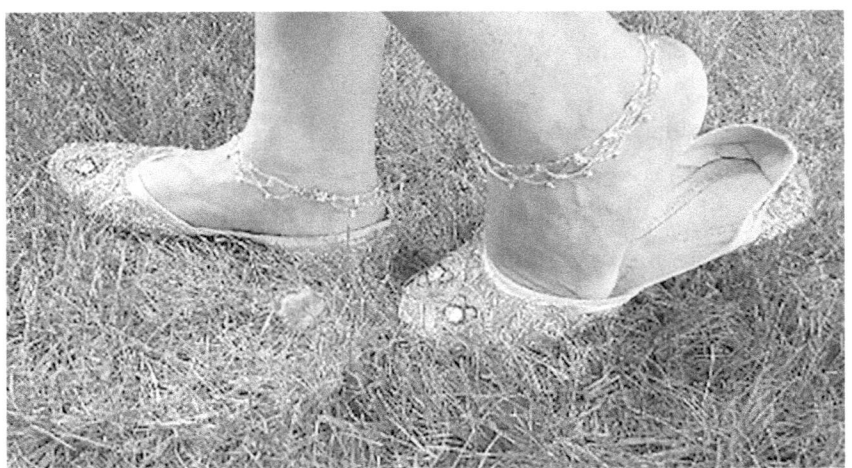

I asked Jugnu " What is that "Chan" "Chan" "Chan" "Chan"?".

Jugnu told that the sound of " Chan" "Chan" "Chan" "Chan" was the sound of pair of Pazeb which she had put in her both legs

In India females used to put the pair of Pazeb in their both feet. Pazeb means chain. It was made of metal like gold or silver. When female used to walk while walking, the chain used to make sounds like "Chan" "Chan" "Chan" "Chan". because some small bell used to attach to the chain when they walk bells rings and produces sound "chan" "chan" " chan" " chan".

I questioned to Jugnu " do you know something about ghost? Ghost legs always be opposite in direction?"

Jugnu told "Yes I know ".

I asked him again that you have seen her legs?

Jugnu told "yes, when I looked back I saw her legs firstly".

I asked Jugnu "what you have seen?".

Jugnu said" yes, both were opposite.

I asked Jugnu, "How old, she looked?".

Jugnu told that she was looking 20 or 22 years old.

I and my sister (NoorJahan) told him to explain all the incident from the beginning in detail. Jugnu told us that incident briefly. He told that he was sick from last seven days. He woke up from the bed today only. He told that before seven days he was returning to his house after attaining the function which was in his uncle's house. While walking on the way, near to his house he realized somebody is following him and he heard sound from backside of him. The sound was "Chan" "Chan" "can" "Chan". He was alone on the way and nobody was walking on the way, the time was 2:30 midnight. Jugnu told that he turned his face back after hearing the sound. He put down his sight on her feet suddenly, when he turned his face back. He saw that both legs were opposite in direction.

In India, some people believes that ghosts legs use to be opposite in direction.

When Jugnu looked back, that lady ghost came very fast near to him. She was very pretty and young, she had fair complexion, big and black eyes, black and long hairs, and straight nose. She was slim and tall. She wore yellow sharara and dupatta, she covered her head with dupatta and she had put old style jewelry and she was looking as a princess. When she came near to Jugnu she told some lines. The lines were that "If you marry me I will transfer my "Old Palace" on your name". She was communicating him in a horrible manner. Her voice and accent were very horrible. Jugnu told that he recognized her that she is lady ghost not a lady by seeing her appearance and horrible voice. He told he scared and started walking very fast but the lady ghost was continuously following him. Jugnu came to his house and led down on his bed and he got high fever over seven days. After seven days Jugnu came to my house and told the incident to me and Noor Jahan.

After hearing the incident of lady ghost from Jugnu. I were terrified all over night because I am afraid of ghosts. Jugnu also told that somebody has seen that same lady ghost front of your house. After hearing that somebody saw that lady ghost near to my house I became very scared and terrified overnight. Nobody believes in ghosts in my house my parent believes in the existence of ghosts but they thinks that ghosts used to be in forests, they do not roam in a city. I and my sister Noor Jahan use to think that ghosts can roam anywhere. So, I and Noor Jahan both became very scared and we told the incident of ghost to our parent. My parent told that Jugnu is telling lies ghosts does not roam they use to live outside the city where people does not live.

I remember that night I and my sister (Noor Jahan) were terrified all over night and did not sleep all night.

I was thinking that somebody have seen the lady ghost, roaming near to my house that lady ghost can come inside also. If lady ghost was roaming outside the house she can come inside also. So, I was terrified all over night.

Next day my brother told me one incident, he told that last night four friends were walking on the way and that lady ghost contact one boy and told that if you marry me I will transfer my" Old Palace" on your name. After hearing these lines from lady ghost that boy fell on ground and rest of three took him to hospital and admitted him.

According to my view some body can see the ghosts some cannot, it depends on their zodiac signs. After admitted the boy to hospital he was medicated some days and discharged from hospital.

Next day I heard something new, which was related to that same lady ghost. I heard from somebody that the lady ghost is came from the bottle, which was broken from the construction land during construction. The bottle was buried inside the land, during the construction one labor had put the rod inside the land the rod touched the bottle and bottle was broken and the spirit came out, which was inside the bottle. The spirit took the appearance of princess.

That construction land was near to my house. People of the city were terrified all over night and they were discussing from each other's. People were discussing each other that who is she? Why she wants to transfer the Old Palace to anybody? Why she is contacting only unmarried boys? What is the relation of Old Palace with her? What is wrong with her? Why she is proposing of marriage? She did not get marriage in her life? What is her psychological problem?

During those days, my relatives came to my house for staying some days. So, that relatives and my sister (Noor Jahan) including me were discussing each other about that lady ghost. My cousins told that her desire of marriage might not fulfil in her life that is why she is roaming and proposing of marriage of herself after her death. During the discussion, I realized something that the spirit must be the spirit of Princess Shabnam. She used to live in" Old Palace". she was the daughter of king of Hyderabad city. Princes Shabnam was unmarried till her death. Her desire of marriage was not fulfilled because of the financial conditions of her father that is why she is proposing of her marriage to beachelor boys and offering the" Old Palace". She might be suffering with psychological problems of marriage and wealth in her life. King of Hyderabad lost his empire during his last days. Only two palaces were left one is "Old Palace" and another one is" New Palace". Princess Shabnam used to live in" Old Palace".

People of old age used to say that the King of Hyderabad city used to live in" Old Palace" with his wife and three children. After the death of King. his daughter Princess Shabnam left alone. she used to live alone in Old Palace, with her servant and one Victoria man I think so, I know the experience of loneness I also used to live alone in my house in India. I used think that my life is like a unrest spirit.

One day Princess Shabnam told to victoria man to take her in Victoria outside the city. Victoria man told her to sit in Victoria and took her away outside the city. When Victoria man took Victoria in outside the city. in jungle. Princess Shabnam told Victoria man to stop the Victoria. he stopped the Victoria and Princess Shabnam got down from Victoria and started walking in jungle. there was one lake in jungle. Princess Shabnam went near to that lake and jumped inside the lake, and she committed suicide. Her body did not get to any one, and not buried, that is why her spirit was there in that lake. So, her soil is not in rest. Old palace" was locked. After Princesses Shabnam jumped in a lake. Victoria man came back to old palace and told that incident to Princesses Shabnam 's servant and both of them decided to go to police and complain, and they went to police and told them to search Princesses Shabnam or her dead body. police went near to that lake and searched. her dead body was not find .so police locked old palace.

India got independence in the year 1947. Before independence India was not India. not a one country. One king used to rule on one or more than one cities and villages. So, in India, many kings used to rule in different parts of countries. After independence, the rule of kings in India was over and India became one country. The government of India has changed into monarchy into democracy. So, the king of Hyderabad city Irfan Ali Khan lost his empire. He had to give all his wealth to government, only two palaces were left "Old Palace "and "New Palace".

King Irfan Ali Khan used to live in" Old Palace" with his first wife and three children. He arranged the marriage of his both sons but did not arrange the marriage of his daughter Princess Shabnam. King loves his daughter very much, he used to search the groom for her daughter in royal family. King Irfan Ali Khan did not have money for dowry. Nobody wanted to get marry to Princess Shabnam without dowry.

In India dowry system is practicing from olden days till now. Dowry system means the father of bride has to give some fund or property to the groom or parent of groom. If the groom belongs to high class family, father of bride had to give more fund or property to them. King Irfan Ali Khan did not have that much money to give to the groom who belong to royal family that is why he was unable to arrange the marriage of his daughter Princesses Shabnam.

I think Princess Shabnam was suffering with depression during her last days. she died in depression only, and not buried that is why the spirit of Princess Shabnam was not in peace and it is unrest and roaming and proposing for her marriage and offering the" Old Palace " as a dowry because in her life she did not have lot of money during marriage time, only Old Palace was left. The desire of marriage was not fulfilled in her life that is why she wants to get marriage after death.

People of old age used to say that they have seen Princess Shabnam. she was quite pretty. he had fair complexion. big and black eyes, straight nose, black and long hairs, she was slim and tall.

She used to wear shararas and dupattas and she used to cover her head with dupatta, in olden days there was custom for females in India to cover the head with dupatta, she used to put jewelries and put the pair of pazeb (chain) in both legs.

After one year of independence King Irfan Ali Khan died and he left two palaces. Princess Shabnam used to live in "Old Palace" with her mother Queen Shakeela . After some year of death of King Irfan Ali Khan Queen also died princess Shabnam left alone in Old Palace. All servants were go away from the old palace. Only one maid and one Victoria man left in "Old palace".

Second palace named " Nayi Haveli ". In that palace wife of king Irfan Ali Khan and their children used to live, but nobody is there in that Palace. It is locked now King Irfan Ali Khan is died and rest of people of that palace like wife of king and their children goon some where they goon i do not know.

In "old Palace " Princess Shabnam used to live with her one servant named Zohra and one Victoria man named Asif, after the death of her parent. some fund left from the empire of her father king Irfan Ali khan, not the fund but some articles like jewelries made up of gold and diamond and some articles to which her father king Irfan Ali khan decorated the palace. Princess Shabnam used to sell those things for her survival and from that amount she used to pay salaries to her servant and Victoria man.

King Irfan Ali Khan was very good in characters and everything. He used to develop the city and used to work for its progress. He was very justifying man and used to do all duties towards people of city and his family members. But his sons were not like him, he was unhappy with them in his life.

After the death of King Irfan Ali Khan, his two sons settled in Paris with their wives and children, and Princess Shabnam was left in "Old Palace". All the servants left their jobs and went away from the palace because she could not pay for them. Only one servant was left and one Victoria man was left. Princess Shabnam was alone in "Old Palace" in her last days. She was unhappy in her last days and became mentally sick. According to my view loneliness use to be very bad that is why she fell in hyper depression.

"Victoria"

There was one Victoria in" Old Palace ", Princess Shabnam used to go for shopping in that Victoria.

Victoria means one horse attached to trolley and pull the trolley and Victoria man use to sit front side of trolley and people use to sit back side of trolley. The Victoria man control the horse and makes him to run and give direction to horse to pass the distance

One day, Princess Shabnam told Victoria man to take her in Victoria outside the city. After going outside the city, she told Victoria man to stop the Victoria and, she left the Victoria and started walking in a jungle. One lake was there in jungle she went near the lake and jumped inside the lake. She committed suicide, like that. Nobody got her body and nobody buried her body, that is why her spirit was not in rest. Nobody were interesting in her life and death, so nobody tried to know about her and tried to search her dead body.

According to my view if the dead body of anyone will not buried the spirit will ben earth and if the dead body of someone will buried, the spirit will go up, in another world.

After the long time of death of Princess Shabnam, one man was passing from the same jungle and suddenly, he got thirsty, he looked left side and right side, he saw one lake in jungle. That was the same lake in which Princess Shabnam committed suicide, he went near the lake and drunk the water from the lake, then the spirit of Princess Shabnam covered the body of that man suddenly. After drinking the water, he went away from the jungle and completed his work, for what he was going from the jungle. After completed the work he come back to Hyderabad. One day his parent came to know that his body is covered by spirit because of his abnormal behavior. So, they contact "Mulla".

"Mulla" is a man who caught the spirit." Mulla" coughed the spirit which has covered on his body and put the spirit in one bottle of glass and put the cap and buried inside the land. That land was near to my house.

In 1994 the owner of the land sold that land to another man. The man who purchase that land started construction to build the complex on it. During the construction, the bottle was broken which was buried inside the land and the spirit of Princess Shabnam came outside the bottle and was roaming.

The people of Hyderabad were very terrified and were discussing each other, they came to one conclusion. They decided to contact the "mulla'. So, they contact to "mulla" and told him to be caught the spirit of lady ghost. And the " Mulla" caught the spirit of lady ghost and put inside the bottle and closed it with cap and buried inside the land which was located outside the city. The people of Hyderabad city were in peace because after that the lady ghost was not seen by anyone. Construction on that land was going on and completed. Now complex is there on that land.

In 1994, I completed 3 years degree in India and I was trying for suitable job. I did not get the suitable job because India was not much developed, those days. During those days, there were not much companies in India that is why I did not get the suitable job and I was doing odd jobs. In 1996, I went to Agra and see the Taj Mahel. Taj Mahel is situated in north side of India my city Hyderabad is located in south side of India. I went to Agra by train distance of 24 hours. I saw the Taj Mahel and I liked it. It is made of marble stones. king Shahjahan who was ruled on Agra and Delhi was built Taj Mahel in love memory of his wife Mumtaz Mahel. Both are buried inside the Tai Mahel.

"Taj Mahal"

From 1996, Hyderabad city was start developing but not much developed to that everyone had a job so there was unemployment problem in India and also in Hyderabad city. I did not have the suitable job while doing the odd job I was surviving myself. Before 2000 nobody had the cellphones in India, but now everyone has cellphones. Only few had cars but now everyone had cars. If the people had to go near, they had to go by walk or they had to go far, they had to hire the taxi. I also did not have cellphone and car in my childhood. I used to go by walk if I had to go near, and when I had to far, I used to hire taxi, during those days.

Year 1997, was not good for me because I was unhappy, during those days, I did not have any suitable job and did not have any man in my life. I belong to high class family, my all uncles and unties are in good positions, here in USA. In 1969 my uncle (father's brother) came to USA. He is builder here. Rest of my family members are also on high position here. When they visited to India, they used to arrange functions for celebrating their victories, I used to attain their functions and think that I will also arrange functions like that and celebrate my victory, while attaining their functions, I was unhappy because I used to realize that they can celebrate I cannot because I did not success to get my goal of my life, my goal of life is make myself up to them. I and my family means my parent and brothers and sister used to live ordinary life during those days. I used to think that I will live life like them tomorrow. but the tomorrow did not come. Then I used to search man who help to get my life goal.

Many men wanted to get marriage to me but I cannot get, because I wanted the man who help me to get my goal of life. So, I was single at that time. I and my family means my parent and brothers and sister used to live in India by birth, my parent, both used to do the jobs and we used to study and used to live ordinary life, other family members used to live luxurious lives so I used to think that in future I will live life like them, not again ordinary. I was living unhappy life even though I used to go for shopping and attaining the functions of my relatives, and used to go to picnic spots I was not enjoying the life. Till that time, my brother became engineer and earn money support us. life became some good more than middleclass not luxurious. In November of 1998 one man and his parent came to my house and proposed to me for marriage to their son. My parent talked to his parent and arranger the marriage, that man did not talk to me only I saw him. They belonged to royal family.

In 1999, I got married with handsome man. I was in India in 1999, he was also in India. He was very good looking. He was fair and tall. After marriage, I was not happy because I did not understand him, His lifestyle was different from my lifestyle and I was not able to cooperate him. He had different hobbies and I had different hobbies.

My fault was that I did not meet him before marriage and did not talk me did not asked about his hobbies and lifestyle because I belong to traditional and cultural family and in my family people does not use to meet each other, parents of both girl and boy use to talk each other and arrange marriage, So, my parent talked to his parent and arrange my marriage. After marriage, both did not understand each other .so both were unhappy with marriage and the marriage was unsuccessful

After one year and three months of marriage we both separated. It was my bad luck. I was shocked and fell in depression on account of breaking marriage, I used to live with my parent, again I used to live unhappy life, in 2001 my parent arranged my sister marriage and she got marriage After some days of my sister's marriage my parent migrated United State of America from India. In 2002, my sister gave birth to one female child named baby Sara, her face was resembled to my face she was very fair and her eyes wear very beautiful and she had beautiful hairs when she born I was very happy by seeing her.

When baby Sara born, my parent visited to India and stay for two years and came to America. I was alone in house because my brothers settle in their lives and sister also had settle in her life. In 2002, my sister came to my house and gave baby Sara to me to look after her and went doing for job in Dubai.

I love baby Sara very much and I used to live with her in my parent house alone with one servant. I got some interest in life because of baby Sara. She was very pretty just like a doll. I liked her very much. She was two years old that time. I used to look after her, but life was very difficult for me, that time. Baby Sara also used to like me, now also she uses to like me. During those days, I am in India and my parent wear in America and they filed me for immigration of United State of America, for my sister also including baby Sara, they were filed for immigration. I used to miss my parent, brothers and sister. I used to miss my rest of family also like my uncles, unties, and cousins. It was very bad time, in bad time, I was trying for good. I got the experience of loneliness. My life was stopped then, it was not running. My experience of loneliness is like that life will look very long time will not pass, experience of stopped the life is that if the life stopped in one place its look very difficult.

My aim of life to migrate United State of America. Now my dream came true. when I was a child I was very sensitive and emotional but my will power was very strong I want to go to America from India. From the younger age, I was trying to go to America. After my divorce, my parent wear migrated to America and they were trying me to migrate America but it takes many years me to come here. That years were very hard for me. I used to think that I am a failure person. My marriage was un success and I do not have any kid. I was a single I used to feel alone. My parent wear far from me and I left my husband, so, I was completely alone during those days. I was suffering with depression. From the childhood, I am most believer of God so that I used to think that God examining me.

I think that God is testing me. From 1994 there was a a bad time in my life. In the year 1994, I completed my education. In the year 1994, I was searching the job but I did not get it. There was no man in my life. I did not have any interest in my life and world. That time was very bad for me. After passing the heard time I saw one man in the year 1998, He was very handsome I was very happy to get married him. I got married in 1999. After married I used to love him very much. I thought that good time has come, in my life, but it was a bad time for me because. Both tendencies wear very different. That's made me very dificuily to adjust with him. Married life became unhappy. He was a dancer and singer, He used to sing songs and dance in functions not in movies. I like songs and dance but sonly songs and dance would not help me to reach my goal.

After getting marriage we both wear unhappy with each other. Both hobbies wear different. Watching of horror movies, TV serial and reading of horror stories are my great bobbies but he like to watch the violence movies and I do not like to watch the violence, so, we do not used to watch TV together and could not discuss on any topic. So, both took the decision of separation. In 2001, we both separated with each other. I did not have any kit also. So, I used to feel bad. There was a frustration in my life. I fell in depression, I was completely alone after separation. There was nothing in my life no job no man and no kid. I was totally alone. All these are what God examine me according to my view. One brother was settle in Canada, he used to support me in my bad time for sending some money from there. Elder other settled in Dubai. My elder brother also used to send some money from Dubai for my survival. Sometimes my sister from Dubai used to come to my house and sometime my elder brother used to come to my house, staying for some days., then I used to feel good.

I and baby Sara used to enjoy with, sometimes with my sister, sometimes with my brother. We both used to go for watching movie with them. Sometimes we both used to go to any picnic spot like zoological park or museum. Sometimes they used to come together from Dubai and sometimes they used to come separately, when they used to come I and baby Sara used to enjoy but when they wear goon we both used to became upset. I wanted to live life like my relative, and that was unwanted life even though used to perform all duties towards my niece baby Sara. I used to give bath and dress up to baby Sara and take her to shopping centers, restaurant, picnic spots and movies. I used to cook food at home for me and baby Sara. I used to play with her and used to sing songs and used to dance for her. Baby Sara used to enjoy with that. Baby Sara started talking from 2 years of age and she was very talkative child, so, I used to enjoy also.

Year 2005 was also a bad year for me. baby Sara became 3 years old, I used to play with her and to exhibition, and purchase the toys for her, And I used to take her to amusement parks also and try to make her happy. In my child hood, I was not happy because my parent did not have much money to buy more toys for us. So, they did not use buy any toy for me and my brothers and sister. Only one or two times in a year they used to buy toys for us and they used to think that if we will play with toys we will not get the time for studies. My parent both are educated that is the reason they wanted us to study more. They did not even take us to any picnic spot. Only one or two times in a year they took us. Going of picnic spot is the wasting of time in my parent's view. According to my view if children will happy they will study well. I used to provide all those things which I did not get in my child hood.

When I was a child I did not have toys when I grow up I did not have children. when I used to buy toys for my nice it was not enough for me some pain was there in my heart. From the childhood, I used to love babies but I did not have baby, I was unhappy for not having the children. I used to treat my niece as my daughter but I used to feel that I do not have child. In the year 2006 baby became 4 years old and used to go to school I used to drop her to school and take her from school. I used to cook food for her and serve her before going the school and coming the school. My friend used to stay near my house her name was' Fatima' she was my good friend. Sometimes I used to take my niece to my friend 's house. She used to give me some moral support to me. I and my niece used to feel good in her house.

In the year 2007 my niece became 5 years old. I and my niece both were alone at home. We both used to stay at that house where I used to stay in childhood. In my childhood, my parent used to go for job and my brothers and sister and I used to go to schools and colleges. Life was going systematically. After that there was no routine in life. In 2008 my life was same. My niece was very intelligent. She was study well. When I went her school to her teachers used to appreciate her. She used to participate all the programs in her school and win all of that when I was a child I did not participate any program in school because I was shy in nature and I was not intelligent. Only good in studies but not very good. My niece was very pretty and intelligent I loved her very much but I am not happy because my life was like a hallow box and life was not running it stopped on one place. I only know that the pain that the life stopped at one place

I born in educated family. My parent. uncles and unties all were highly educated. In my childhood, I was very sensitive and emotional but my will power was very strong. When I was growing I used to think that I will also study. My uncles and aunties and cousins all were in America and my parent and my brothers and sister were in India. I also wanted to migrate America. When I was grown up I got education but my goal was far from me.

In 2008 my life was full of frustration and irritation. My life was in darkness but I used to see light far from me. I and my niece still left alone at the home. I used to perform all duties towards my niece and anyone and live the unwanted life. I was also traditional. I used to think that if traditions are in life, life will become interesting. So, I used to perform all duties and traditions and my life was going like that. In the year the problems were same.

My hobbies are reading, cooking and watching of old Hindi movies and old songs. Reading of horror stories and watching of horror movies and TV serials are my great hobbies. So, there was a problem of passing of time in those days from that time because I divorced to my husband in the year was 2004. Sometimes I used to read the articles which were given in newspapers and sometimes. I used to watch the old Hindi movies and old Hindi songs on TV and sometimes I used to perform the traditions and sometimes I used to watch horror TV serials along with baby Sara Sometimes, I used to read horror stories, and used to cook food, time was passing like that. Because my parent wear trying to migrate America during those days, there was some light in my dark life that light make a stick for me which support me to walk on the way where I was going in darkness of life when my niece was growing she was becoming my friend. I used to communicate her and we both used to go to restaurants and shopping. My niece (baby Sara) is very intelligent girl. she used to talk to me in a good manner and I used to enjoy her company

In the year 2008 the problems were same in my life. And year 2009 and year 2010 were like that only in year 2011, there was chances of getting US visa. In 2012, Finally I got the US visa on immigration base I became little happy to see the visa. On 18 October 2012, I left India and I reached America on 19 October 2012. my desire for life is going to fulfill and my dream was going to come true. That day I was very scared because first time I took the international flight so I was very scared in a plane. When it reached to America I became happy. When the plane is near the airport, I looked down from the window, there was very beautiful view near Chicago airport. That is first time I saw America. Houses were looking very small and beautiful and cars were looking very beautiful and small from the flight. So, the plane was landed I came out of plane to airport that was Chicago airport

Actually, my family used to stay at Minnesota so I took the plane from India to Chicago, and from Chicago I had to take the connective flight of Minnesota. I was very happy when I was in Chicago airport because there I became US immigrant. After getting the stamp on my passport of immigration I was telling the news to my family members of becoming US immigrant by cell phone. That was a remembering day of life. The date was 19 October 2012, 2 o clock after noon. Connective flight was at 10.30 PM. I had to wait for a long time on Chicago airport to take the flight of Minnesota. At 10.30 pm, I took the flight on Chicago airport, the flight which was going to Minnesota. The flight was land on 11.30 pm on Minnesota. After that my family members came to airport and receive me from airport and we all came to our house at 12.00 pm.

Next day my family members and I went for shopping and I watch some places in Minnesota. That places were very beautiful. Day by day I used to watch the different places of America and I used to say in mind that the country is very beautiful. It is just like heaven. Heaven of the land. Beginning days of mine in US the climate was not very cold, little cold. I used to see the roads while going for shopping and restaurants, different varieties and colors of flowers are there and they were very beautiful. I like flowers. After some days, the climate became very cold I used to feel very cold because I came from the hot place. India is not very hot but little hot. In 2012 the climate of America was very cold. For the reason that India is hot I am not in a habit to face the cold climate. That was the first year for me in America. It was very cold climate. But I like United State of America.

The problems were same in the year 2012 also, I did not get any job. I was searching the man to marry and job to earn, through internet. In the year 2013 the problems were same. Life was full of frustration. No one problem has solved. In 2014 the problems were same. Activities were also same. I saw searching job and man. In the year 2015, I got one man through internet. He was in India. I decided to marry him. On November 2015, I went India and met him and came back to America on 2016 He is good in characters and nature. Now the question is I reach my goal or not? NO not yet. My goal is still far from me. My goal of life was that 'I wanted me to progress as much as my uncles and aunties. Now he is in India he has to come to US and I hope that I reach my goal, because he is educated and heard working man. I am trying him to comes to United State of America.

In 2016 I visited to India for few months and met him. he enjoyed to met each other. In 2017 I tried for earning, so I arranged one small business from home and I was earning some money, not much, little amount, I was not happy but it makes some help in my survival. In my house where I use to live in, is my mom house and my brother use to earn money and arrange food and all things for our mom and for me and also himself.

In 2018 I fell ill and the Doctor suggest the surgery of stomach because one tumor was their in my stomach, I did not want surgery .So I requested the Doctor to prescribe medication not the surgery and Doctor done the same, after some months I realized that I did by medication, during those my citizenship of United State of America was in processing, so I decided that after taking the citizenship I will take the date of surgery. in 2019 I decides for surgery and told the Doctor to give date for surgery and Doctor had give the date and my surgery was done in given date, that is January 2019.

After my surgery, after taking of few weeks bed rest I started trying for that man to get the visa of United State of America and I visited India and meet him again and after staying few months in India I came back to Unites State of America at December 2019, next day was 1 January 2020 here and then I was trying for earning and I got one part time job here and was getting some little amount. Now is one small business and one part time job now and getting some money I am little happy now.

In march 2020 I heard one corona virus case in Minnesota in news, From till date I am unhappy because the processing of that man of getting visa was stopped and also I was facing other difficulties.

That is the first experience of my life, that the virus spreads all over the world. In my childhood I used to hear that one village or one city used to infected with one disease like plague or diarrhea. I was in India in my childhood.

My father used to say that, in his childhood one whole city or village used to effect with disease. but in my life no one disease or virus spread in the city or village and now corona virus spread all over the world.

During lockdown I used to cook food and eat watch the You tube, videos of music and cooking and video of gaining knowledge and horror movies and horror TV serials on You tube, after lockdown I am doing the same even though I am doing these things I use to be very frustrate and my heart is full of fear, .now vaccine has came in december2020.

Corona virus is also made me difficulties to achieve my goal. even though I am facing the difficulties and life failure I did not take any alcoholic drugs and always I use to try again and again and my massage to all people that try again and again to achieve the goal because some times the lock will open with last key of the keychain like that your lock of fortune will open with the last key your effort.

www.ingramcontent.com/pod-product-compliance
Lightning Source LLC
LaVergne TN
LVHW021736060526
838200LV00052B/3311